Be a Star like Angelina!

Children from 3 years old can now be a little ballet star with big dreams!

The Angelina Ballerina Dance Academy offers classical ballet classes following and bringing to life the adventures of Angelina Ballerina.

The Angelina Ballerina Dance Academy introduces children to classical ballet, through fun and endearing stories. They encourage little girls to become budding ballerinas.

Ballet is so much fun!

For further information and to book a free trial class please call Littlemagictrain on 01865 739048 or visit www.littlemagictrain.com
Please quote REF: ABA08

www.angelinaballerina.com

This
Angelina Ballerina
Annual belongs to

....

....

Angelina Ballerina™

Annual 2008

Contents

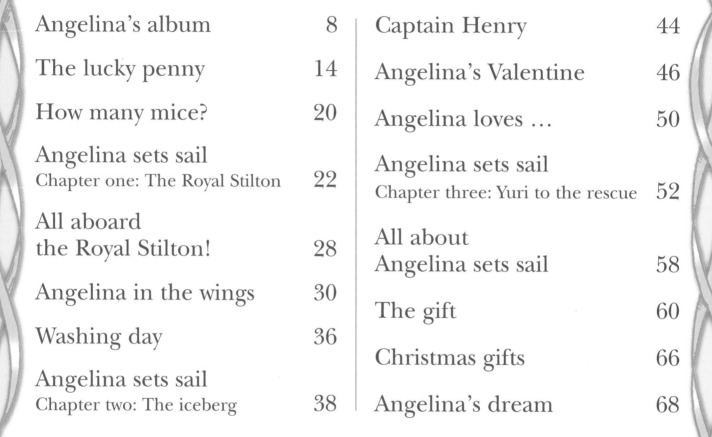

EGMONT
We bring stories to life

First published in Great Britain 2007
by Egmont UK Limited, 239 Kensington High Street,
London W8 6SA

Stories adapted from original scripts by Laura Beaumont,
Paul Larson and Jan Page.

Do you want to know a secret? I'm going to be a famous ballerina one day! I know I'll have to work hard to make my dream come true, but I know I can do it, with the help of my teacher, Miss Lilly!

"Bravo, my darlink!"

Angelina's album

Do you have a camera? I do, and I just love taking photographs! I keep them in my special secret photo album. I only ever let my very best friends look at it with me. Luckily, that includes you!

My dad **Maurice** owns the Chipping Cheddar newspaper.

Dad

Dad loves playing the fiddle!

Mum's name is **Matilda**. She's always got a big hug for me.

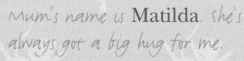
Mum

Mum's Cheddar cheese pies are yummy!

Polly is my baby sister. I wonder if she'll love ballet when she grows up?

I can't wait until she's big enough to dance with me.

I like **Grandpa**'s scary stories – as long as I've got his paw to hold!

Grandma spends hours sewing ribbons and beads on to my ballet dresses.

My best friend **Alice** does better
cartwheels than anyone – even me!

she's always on the go!

Alice

Alice loves me, books – and cheesy nibbles.

sammy

My school friend **Sammy** likes playing tricks on people.

Henry *is my little cousin. He's sweet!*

Henry

William

William *loves ballet almost as much as I do.*

Penelope *and* **Priscilla** *are in my ballet class, but they're not my friends. They're really sneaky!*

The Pinkpaws Twins

Miss Lilly *is my hero. she's the best ballet teacher in the world, and she's teaching me everything she knows.*

Miss Lilly

When you have a teacher like Miss Lilly you just can't help working hard.

i'm very proud to be her "darlink"!

Alice took this photo of me. She said I just had to put it into my secret album because it's so ... ME! What do you think?

This space in my secret photo album is for my new friend – that's YOU! Put your photograph in the frame, or draw a picture of yourself, then write your name on the line.

Friends forever!

This is my new friend

....

The lucky penny

1 Angelina and Alice were on the way to ballet class. "The film of the Swan Princess ballet is on!" said Angelina. "And we're going after class!"

2 Angelina skipped along happily. "Where's your hair bow?" asked Alice. "I don't know," said Angelina. "I'll look for it later."

3 In class, Angelina danced well, but her landing was a bit wobbly. "Darlink, do it like Priscilla!" said Miss Lilly. That made Angelina cross!

4 At the end of class Miss Lilly said, "You must be here on time tomorrow for the Theatre Royal auditions. Good luck, darlinks!"

5 "I'm not coming to see the film," Angelina told Alice. "I'm going home to practise for tomorrow. You and Henry can go without me."

6 Angelina dropped her bag near a puddle and picked up a penny. "It must be a lucky penny!" said Alice. "It stopped your bag getting wet."

7 Angelina picked something else up. "My hair bow!" she said. "This penny really is lucky! I don't need to practise now. Come on, the film starts soon!"

8 Angelina, Alice and Henry went to the village hall to see the film. Angelina showed Henry her lucky penny. "I've got a jar full of those!" he said.

9 "But the numbers on mine are the year I was born," said Angelina. She tossed the lucky penny into her bag, but it rolled away without her seeing!

10 After the film Alice said, "Maybe you should do some practice for tomorrow?" But Angelina shook her head. "I don't need to now. Watch me!"

11 Angelina twirled and leapt, but she fell over and landed, **thump!** "Now why did that happen?" she said. "I need my lucky penny!"

12 She looked in her bag. "It's gone!" she said. "That's why I can't do the steps properly. Help me look for it, you two! I've got to find that penny."

13 They looked everywhere, but they didn't find the penny. They ran back to the village hall but it was locked! Then Henry found a loose bit of wood.

14 "I can't fit through," said Angelina. "Will you try, Henry?" Henry nodded and squeezed inside. He came out with lots of things, but not the lucky penny.

15 "Sorry," he said as they walked home. "It's not your fault," said Angelina. "I just wish I had my lucky penny for the ballet tomorrow."

16 They met the Pinkpaws twins. "Not practising, Angelina?" asked Penelope. "She doesn't need to!" said Henry. "She's got a lucky penny!"

17 "Let's see it!" said Priscilla. Alice told her that it was lost. "Well, **I** don't need luck," said Priscilla, dancing around. "We'll see!" said Angelina.

18 Angelina started to practise as soon as she got home. She did her steps over and over again, until it was dark and the house was quiet.

19 When Angelina got to Miss Lilly's next morning, Henry put a coin in her paw. "My lucky penny!" she said. "You found it, Henry!"

20 Everyone waited in line to dance for Miss Lilly. They were very nervous but Angelina wasn't worried because she had her lucky penny!

21 Priscilla danced first, then it was Angelina. There was no doubt who the best dancer was – Angelina! She would dance at the Theatre Royal.

22 Later, in Henry's bedroom, Angelina gave him a big hug and swung him up in the air. "Where did you find my lucky penny?" she asked.

23 Henry reached under his bed and pulled out a jar full of pennies. "I told you," he said. "I've got LOTS of lucky pennies. I gave you one of mine!"

24 Angelina laughed and gave the penny back to Henry. "I'm going to be **very** lucky now, aren't I?" he said. Angelina smiled. "You really are, Henry!"

"Mum, your Cheddar cheese pie tastes better than anything in the whole wide world!" says Angelina. "Will you teach me how to make it?"

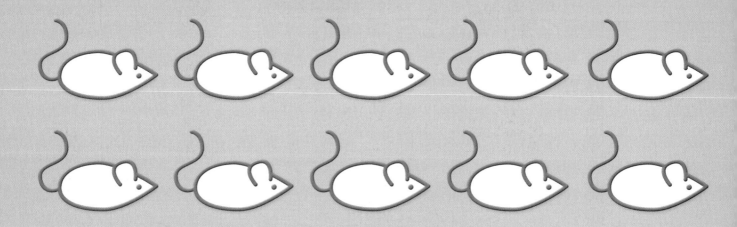

Look at the picture on the next page. Can you see where the little grey mice are hiding?

Colour in a mouse above for each grey mouse you can see. Then count the ones you have coloured, and circle the number.

1 2 3 4 5 6 7 8 9 10

ANSWER: There are 8 little grey mice.

Angelina sets sail

Chapter one: The Royal Stilton

Miss Lilly watched as Angelina did a perfect double spin. She clapped her hands. "Bravo, my darlink!" she said.

"But it was only a double spin," said Angelina. "I wanted to do a triple."

"Oh, you are an impatient little mouseling, Angelina!" said Miss Lilly. "It took me many years to learn to do a triple spin!"

"Bravo, my darlink!"

Miss Lilly had exciting news for Angelina and the other mouselings. Her old friend Mr Operatski had asked them to dance at the Dacovia Festival of Dance. "Oh, they will love you!" said Miss Lilly.

"Oh, it's beautiful!"

Soon it was time to pack. Mrs Mouseling showed Angelina the lovely new ballet dress she had made. "And this is for good luck," she said, giving her a little box.

Inside was a necklace with a tiny ballerina on it! "Oh, it's beautiful!" said Angelina.

The Royal Stilton

Miss Lilly and the mouselings went to the docks. They were going to sail to Dacovia on a huge ship called the Royal Stilton. "It's bigger than a house!" said Alice.

"Bigger than twenty houses!" said Angelina.

At the docks Miss Lilly met her nephew, Yuri. His job was to look after the radio on the ship.

"Miss Lilly told us about you," Alice told him. "She said you're the best dancer in Dacovia."

Just then a loud horn sounded. "All aboard!" said Yuri. "The Royal Stilton waits for no one!"

"All aboard!"

As they walked along the deck, Miss Lilly spoke to Yuri. "I will talk to the Captain," she said. "He must allow you to marry his daughter."

"Oh, no, please don't say anything, Aunt Lilly," said Yuri. "I must prove myself to him."

They turned a corner and almost bumped into the Captain. He was pleased to see Miss Lilly, but angry

The Captain was angry.

when he saw Yuri. "Back to the Radio Room, Sailor!" he said. "Now!"

Angelina and Alice went to their cabin. "Poor Yuri," said Alice. "I don't think the Captain likes him."

Cards arrived inviting them to the Captain's Welcoming Banquet.

"Look, Alice," said Angelina. "There's a spare one. I know, we'll give it to Yuri! If the Captain sees him dance, he'll let him marry his daughter! Come on!"

"Come on!"

Angelina led Alice along the deck past a sign that said **OFF LIMITS**.

"No one will know," she said.

She put the card under the door of the Radio Room. Then she and Alice hurried away.

When Yuri found the card he read what Angelina had written on it:

"You are requested to dance in honour of Miss Lilly."

Later, the Captain called everyone on deck to take part in a safety drill. He showed the mouselings how to put on their life vests then said, "Any questions?"

Henry put up his paw. "Can I please steer the ship, Mister Captain, Sir?"

The Captain shook his head. He gave Henry a stern look and walked away without replying.

"Can I please steer the ship?"

Priscilla and Penelope Pinkpaws ran after him. "It's an emergency, Captain!" said Priscilla. "We left our new ballet costumes at home!"

"Yes," said Penelope. "We need to use the ship's radio to call Mum so she can send them to us!"

"The ship's radio is for **real** emergencies only," said the Captain. "It's not for sending messages about missing ballet dresses!"

"It's an emergency!"

That night, all the guests went to the Ballroom of the Royal Stilton for the Captain's Welcoming Banquet.

All except the Pinkpaws twins. They had plans to make!

Yuri started dancing.

As the guests chatted, Angelina saw Yuri at the side of the stage. He spoke to the musicians and they started to play a different tune.

Yuri started dancing the Dacovian Sailors' Dance! He stamped and stomped across the stage.

"What a surprise, Captain!" said Miss Lilly.

But the Captain wasn't listening.

Yuri was in big trouble!

He strode to the stage and spoke to the musicians. The music stopped suddenly and Yuri stopped dancing.

"How dare you, Sailor?" said the Captain angrily. "You left your post in the Radio Room without my permission. And all that stamping and stomping could rock the ship! You will be punished for this!"

Angelina looked at Alice. "Oh, no!" she said. "What have I done?"

What will happen to Yuri?

What are the Pinkpaws twins up to?

Find out in **Chapter two: The iceberg**. It starts on page 38.

All aboard the Royal Stilton!

The Captain asked Miss Lilly to be his special guest at the Welcoming Banquet.

1

These pictures look the same, but there are 5 things that are different in picture 2. Can you spot them all?

2

ANSWERS: 1. Angelina's suitcase has changed colour; 2. One of the butterflies on Miss Lilly's dress is missing; 3. The stripes on the Captain's sleeve are missing; 4. Miss Lilly's boots have changed colour; 5. The flowers on Angelina's shoulder bag have disappeared.

"Cheddar Chiffon Surprise or Royal Cheesy Mousse?" said Alice at the Banquet.

"Both, Alice," said Angelina. "BOTH!"

These pictures look the same, but there are 5 things that are different in picture 2. Can you spot them all?

1

2

ANSWERS: 1. One of the bows on the smaller cake has changed colour; 2. The piece of cheese is missing; 3. The cake stand has changed colour; 4. The orange slices in the juice have disappeared; 5. The icing on the little cakes has changed colour.

Angelina in the wings

1 Miss Lilly had exciting news for the mouselings. "Madame Zizi is dancing in the *Sun Queen*. She is coming here with the director, Mr Popoff."

2 There was more news. "One of the sunbeam dancers has mouse pox, so she can't dance," said Miss Lilly. "One of you will take her place."

3 Angelina SO hoped that Madame Zizi would choose her to dance. She couldn't wait to get home to tell Mum and Dad.

4 "But Penelope and Priscilla Pinkpaws already have costumes for the ballet," Angelina told Mum. "Madame Zizi will choose them."

5   "It's not costumes that matter," said Mr Mouseling. "And Henry will be at the audition class. He'll bring you good luck."

6   "WHAT?" said Angelina. "I have to take Henry? The last time he came to class he spilled his drink and Priscilla slipped in it!"

7   "Don't worry, I'm sure that won't happen this time," said Mr Mouseling. Just then Henry's ladybird toy spilled his drink on the table. "I hope!"

8   Next day, Miss Lilly had more news. "Poor Penelope and Priscilla have mouse pox. They will not be able to dance for Madame Zizi," she said.

9 Angelina couldn't help smiling. She turned and whispered to Alice. "Now this sunbeam is really going to shine for Madame Zizi!"

10 Madame Zizi watched as the mouselings danced. She pointed to Angelina. "That leetle mouseling," she said. "Let me see her."

11 Everyone watched Angelina dance. Except Henry! A fly landed on his nose and he dropped his ladybird toy. It set off across the studio floor …

12 The ladybird bumped into Angelina's foot and she fell over! It stopped in front of Madame Zizi. Henry smiled and picked it up.

13 Madame Zizi picked Henry up and stood him on a chair. "Thees leetle mouseling ees a perfect sunbeam. The other one will be his understudy!"

14 When she got back home Angelina burst into tears. "I've got to ... **sob!** ... watch while Henry ... **sob!** ... dances," she said. "It's not fair!"

15 "Make sure Madame Zizi sees how good you are and she'll add another sunbeam," said Alice. Angelina smiled. "You are a GENIUS!" she said.

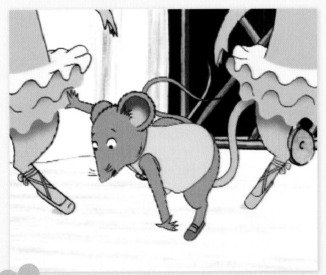

16 Mr Popoff was not pleased with Henry! "The boy dancer is useless," he said. "But the audience will LOVE heem!" said Madame Zizi.

17 Angelina bumped into Henry on her way to the wardrobe room. "Where's the stage?" he asked. "Not now, Henry!" said Angelina. "I'm busy!"

18 Poor Henry was very late! "Eet ees not ees fault!" said Madame Zizi. She lifted Henry into her arms. "Angelina did not look after eem as I told her to!"

19 Angelina and Alice heard Mr Popoff talking to Madame Zizi. "We will have to use the understudy," he told her. "The boy mouseling has to go!"

20 His words made Angelina feel sorry for Henry. "Oh, please give him a chance," she said. "I'll help him." Madame Zizi nodded. "Very well."

21 Angelina worked so hard with Henry that Mr Popoff was very pleased with him. "He is perfect now, thanks to you," he told Angelina.

22 When another dancer got mouse pox, there was good news for Angelina. She and Henry were BOTH going to dance as sunbeams!

23 Next morning, Mrs Mouseling went into Angelina's bedroom with bags of cheesy niblets. "Good morning," she said. Then she stopped and stared!

24 Angelina and Henry were both covered in bright red spots. Now **they** had mouse pox! "Oh, dear," said Mrs Mouseling. "Two little spotty sunbeams!"

Washing day

"I'll help you hang out the washing, Mum!" says Angelina. "I like Dad's new stripy socks!"

Which 3 pieces are missing from the jigsaw on the next page? Draw and colour them in if you like.

ANSWER: Pieces 1, 3 and 5 are missing.

Angelina sets sail

Chapter two: The iceberg

William and Angelina were going to dance together in Dacovia. But when William arrived at class he had a clothes peg on his nose – and three on his tail!

"Why are you dressed up like a washing line, William?" whispered Angelina.

"I get a bit seasick," said William. "Dad gave me a book called *101 Cures for Seasickness*. This is number 17 – and it works!"

When Angelina and William started to dance, the pegs all popped off. "Ooooo-er ..." said William, going green and rushing outside.

"I feel ill!"

"I feel ill!"

After class Angelina and Alice found poor Yuri scrubbing the deck!

"You shouldn't be doing that," said Angelina.

"The Captain thinks I should," said Yuri. "He says I have to make the deck shine – or else!"

*"Make the deck shine
– or else!"*

38

"One shiny deck coming up!"

When Yuri went off to get a new scrubbing brush, Angelina poured a whole box of cleaning powder into his bucket of water.

Alice smiled when she saw the bubbles. "One shiny deck coming up!"

Alice and Angelina had almost finished cleaning the deck when they heard someone coming.

"Quick, hide!" said Angelina.

They watched as the Captain came closer. He slipped on the soapy deck, got tangled up in some ropes, and – **clang!** – the bucket ended up on his head!

Just then, Yuri arrived.

"YOU AGAIN!" said the Captain angrily. "GO!"

"YOU AGAIN!"

"Oh, no, what have I done now?" whispered Angelina.

That night, Angelina went to see Yuri. "I'm sorry!" she told him. "I thought if the Captain saw you dance, and if I made the deck extra shiny, he'd let you marry his daughter. But it went wrong and it's all my fault!"

"But no more helping, OK?"

Yuri wasn't angry at all. "It's all right," he said. "But no more helping, OK?"

"Not the tiniest bit," said Angelina. "I promise!"

Angelina said goodnight and ran back to her cabin. She felt a lot happier now. "Time for a triple spin!" she said. She leapt, turned once … twice … but landed on the deck, **thud!** She didn't notice that her necklace had fallen off!

Next morning, Angelina couldn't find her necklace. She looked everywhere for it.

"It'll turn up," said Alice.

It **did**! The Pinkpaws twins found it when they sneaked off to find the Radio Room!

Thud!

Inside, Yuri got a radio message. There was a big storm coming.

When he left to tell the Captain about the storm, Penelope and Priscilla sneaked into the Radio Room.

"The radio must work like a telephone," said Priscilla, pressing buttons. "Hello, hello?"

She shook the radio. "Hello?" she shouted. "Hellooooooo!"

She gave it a big **whack** – and it fell to pieces!

"You broke it!" said Penelope. "We'll be in BIG trouble when Miss Lilly finds out …"

"You broke it!"

Priscilla smiled. "But **I** didn't break it," she said, putting Angelina's necklace on the floor. "Angelina did!"

The Captain planned to go north to avoid the storm.

"But those seas are frozen," said Yuri. "What about icebergs?"

"I know about icebergs, Sailor!" the Captain said angrily. "Get back to your post!"

"What about icebergs?"

The Royal Stilton sailed into cold, rough seas. It swayed from side to side in the big waves.

Suddenly there was a loud scraping sound. The ship had hit a huge iceberg. It was stuck!

"Don't worry," the Captain told everyone. "We'll use the radio to call for help."

Priscilla and Penelope looked at each other …

The ship was stuck!

"Angelina?"

Miss Lilly followed the Captain to the Radio Room. "I must speak to you about getting a message to Dacovia …" she said.

"And I must speak to you," said the Captain. "One of the mouselings has broken the radio!"

He held up Angelina's necklace as she walked in behind Miss Lilly.

"My necklace!" cried Angelina.

"Angelina?" whispered Miss Lilly …

 Will Angelina be blamed for breaking the radio?
What will happen to the Royal Stilton?

Turn to Chapter three: Yuri to the rescue. It begins on page 52.

Captain Henry

"Some day, I want to be a Captain, just like you. It's the most important job in the whole world – and you're the best Captain EVER!" Henry told the Captain.

That made the Captain smile! "Well, if things get rough, Henry," he said, "I know who to call to help me!"

Things **did** get rough on the Royal Stilton! Can you help Henry steer from the top of the maze to the bottom, without hitting any icebergs?

"Aye, aye, Captain!"

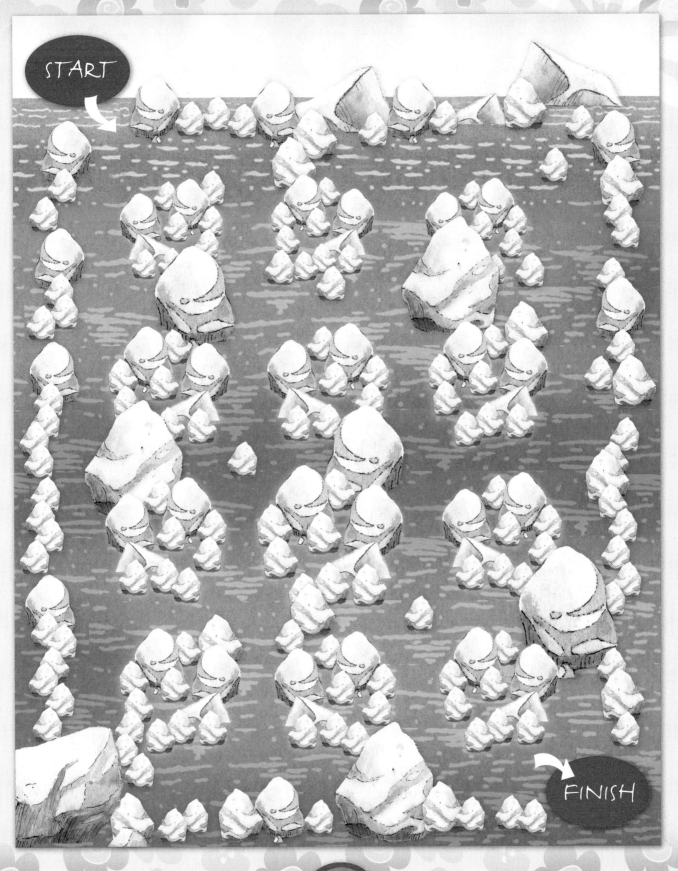

START

FINISH

45

Angelina's Valentine

The little pictures will help you read this story. When you see the pictures of Angelina and her friends, say their names.

Henry

William

Angelina

Miss Lilly

Sammy

made a Valentine card for . bought an extra special card for .

 wrote a message in it.

"Roses are red, violets are blue.

Sugar is sweet,  is too."

 bought flowers for  .

"Are you taking them to her house?"

asked  . "No!"  said.

"  might see me!" So

gave the card and flowers to  .

 thought they were from him!

"Do you like the flowers  sent you?" asked  .

"Yes," said . "But they were from ."  shook his head. "No,  sent them," he told her. "Naughty !" said . "He let me think they were from him!"

Later on,  got a lovely

Valentine card with a big heart on

the front. It said "Edam is red,

Stilton is blue. Cheesecake is sweet,

 is too." "Who sent it?"

said . We know, don't we?

Yes, it was ! But don't tell

, will you? It's our secret!

Angelina loves ...

I love my family, my friends, ballet and ... all sorts of things!

I love ... spring flowers.

I love ... crinkly, crackly autumn leaves.

I love ... sunshine!

I love ... Christmas gifts!

I love ... my baby sister, Polly.

I love ... ballet story books.

I love ... drawing pictures of Miss Lilly.

And I love ... flying. Wheee!

What things do you love? Write your name and some words.

_____ loves ... _____

_____ loves ... _____

_____ loves ... _____

Angelina gasped. "The radio's broken?" she said. "I didn't do it!"

Yuri stepped forward. "That's right," he said. "I did!"

"That's not true!" said Angelina. "It was me!"

"Enough!" said the Captain. "Whoever did it, the radio is broken, and we are stuck on an iceberg!"

"The radio is broken!"

"Angelina did NOT do this," Miss Lilly told the Captain firmly. "And neither did Yuri!"

Miss Lilly took Angelina back to her cabin. "I did go to the Radio Room," said Angelina sadly.

"I know," said Miss Lilly. "You did break the rules, darlink, but not the radio. I know you were trying to help Yuri."

Miss Lilly sighed. "Oh, it is such a shame that I will not see my mouselings dance now ..."

"Oh, it is such a shame ..."

"But we can still dance!" said Angelina. "We can dance right here, on the Royal Stilton, in the ballroom!"

While Angelina made her plans, the Captain had to decide how to free the ship from the iceberg.

Henry went to see him. "I can steer us out of danger," he said. "I know how to do it."

The Captain smiled. He lifted

"Aye, aye, Captain!"

Henry on to the chair in front of the big ship's wheel. "Very well, take the wheel, Henry," he said.

"Aye, aye, Captain!" said Henry.

Soon everything was ready and the ballet was about to begin.

"WHAT?"

"Costumes!" Miss Lilly told Penelope and Priscilla.

"Er, sorry, we left them at home," said Priscilla.

"We tried everything to get them," said Penelope.

"Even the radio ..." said Priscilla.

"WHAT?" cried Miss Lilly. "The radio! It was you two who broke it?"

"Bravo!"

Before she could say any more, the music began. Angelina and William danced their duet and the passengers cried, "Bravo!" Even the Captain!

As they moved across the stage Angelina had an idea. "Keep dancing!" she said to William, and ran off to talk to Yuri.

"Remember how the Captain said your stamping would make the ship rock?" she said. "Bring all the sailors to the ballroom. You need to dance the best Dacovian Sailors' Dance ever! The more stamping the better!"

"Aye, aye!" said Yuri.

"Aye, aye!"

Angelina ran back to the ballroom and asked the musicians to play a different tune. They did, and on to the stage marched Yuri and the other sailors. They danced across the stage, then back again. They stomped and stamped their feet as hard as they  could, and the ship began to rock from side to side.

"... play a different tune."

"The ship's moving!" said Alice.

"Yes, but not enough!" said Angelina. She spoke to the other mouselings. "We have to join in!"

The sailors and the mouselings danced from one side of the stage to the other, STOMP, STOMP!

STOMP, STOMP!

The ship rocked more and more then – **creak! crack!** – it broke away from the iceberg! Everyone cheered and clapped.

Creak! crack!

"You did it, Angelina!" said Yuri.

"Thank you," said the Captain. "I owe you both an apology."

As he spoke the ship rocked again. "Who's steering it?" asked Angelina.

Can you guess? Yes, it was Captain Henry!

In Dacovia, Yuri arrived with flowers for Angelina and Alice. He was dressed in an officer's uniform!

Officer Yuri!

"You didn't have anything to do with the Captain making me an officer and allowing me to marry his daughter, did you?" he asked.

Angelina smiled. "Of course I didn't …"

That evening Angelina danced as she had never danced before. She leapt into the air and turned one … two … three times!

"Of course I didn't …"

"Bravo, Angelina!"

The audience gasped, then clapped and cheered.

"A triple spin!" Yuri said to the Captain's daughter, who sat by his side. "Bravo, Angelina!"

All about
Angelina sets sail

Did you enjoy the **Angelina sets sail** story? Can you answer these questions about it?

 1 Which country did the mouselings sail to?

 2 What did Mum give Angelina as a good luck present?

 3 What was the name of the ship? Was it:
a. the Great Cheddar
b. the Royal Stilton, or
c. the Mighty Mouse?

 4 Who had a book called *101 Cures for Seasickness*?

What did Penelope and Priscilla forget to pack?

Which part of the ship did Yuri work in? Was it:
a. the Galley
b. the Engine Room, or
c. the Radio Room?

Why did the Captain think Angelina had broken the radio?

Angelina danced a duet with Henry. True or false?

Angelina did a triple spin.
How many turns did she make?

Who sat next to Yuri as Angelina danced?

ANSWERS: 1. Dacovia; 2. A necklace; 3. b, The Royal Stilton; 4. William; 5. Their dance costumes; 6. c, the Radio Room; 7. He found her necklace in the Radio Room; 8. False, she danced with William; 9. Three; 10. The Captain's daughter.

The gift

1 The mouselings were all busy getting things ready for the Christmas party at Miss Lilly's ballet school. All except Angelina …

2 She was gazing at Miss Lilly's glass snow dome. When she shook it lots of snowflakes swirled around a tiny figure of a ballerina.

3 "Isn't it lovely?" said Miss Lilly. "My first ballet teacher gave it to me many, many years ago, when I could hardly point my toes!"

4 Just then Doctor Tuttle arrived with a huge Christmas tree. He pulled one end and Mr Mouseling pushed the other. "Heave!"

5 "I can't wait to see the tree when it's decorated and has all our gifts on it," said Alice. "Yes," said Angelina. "I've made my gift for Miss Lilly."

6 Penelope Pinkpaws heard her. "A home-made gift! How sweet," she said. "And we only have an expensive necklace for her!" said her twin sister Priscilla.

7 When Angelina got home she looked sad. "What's wrong?" asked Mum. "It's the picture I painted for Miss Lilly," said Angelina. "It's HOME-MADE!"

8 Angelina emptied her money box and went to the shops with Alice and William. "I'm going to buy the PERFECT present for Miss Lilly," she told them.

9 Angelina found just what she was looking for. It was a big hat with feathers and ribbons and lots of bright, shiny jewels pinned to the front.

10 "It costs sixty-four pounds and ninety-nine pence," the lady in the shop told her. Angelina gasped. She didn't have that much money.

11 On the way home Angelina saw some buskers on the village green. They sang songs then collected money from the people who had been listening.

12 "I've got an idea!" said Angelina. Soon there was more music on the village green. This time it was ballet music – and Angelina was dancing to it!

13 People watched, and at the end of the dance they all gave William some money. Now Angelina had enough money to buy the hat for Miss Lilly!

14 They hurried back to the shop. But the hat had been sold! "Oh, no," said Angelina. "Now what am I going to give Miss Lilly for Christmas?"

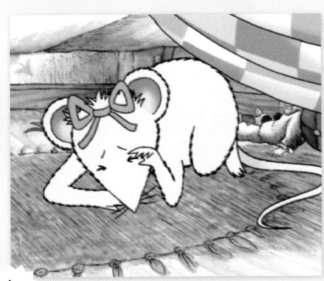

15 On the day of the party Mrs Mouseling found Angelina hiding under her bed! "I'm not going without a special gift for Miss Lilly," she cried.

16 "But you have a special gift for her," said Mrs Mouseling. "Your lovely picture. Imagine how upset Miss Lilly will be if you aren't there to give it to her."

17 All the mouselings sat around the Christmas tree to watch Miss Lilly open her presents. There was one on every branch! But Angelina hid hers!

18 The next gift Miss Lilly opened was the necklace from Penelope and Priscilla. "And don't forget this one," said Priscilla. "It's from Angelina."

19 "Oh, your painting is beautiful!" said Miss Lilly. "Is it?" said Angelina. "Oh, yes," said Miss Lilly. "I love it! I will put it on the wall this minute."

20 Miss Lilly gave Angelina a big hug. "Thank you," she said. "A home-made gift like yours is extra-special. It comes right from the heart!"

21 Angelina was telling Alice what Miss Lilly had said when Mrs Hodgepodge arrived. She was wearing the hat that Angelina had wanted to buy!

22 Everyone stared. It looked a bit silly! "Just look at that hat, darlink!" whispered Miss Lilly. "What a … creation!" Angelina burst out laughing.

23 Angelina didn't open her gift from Miss Lilly until she got home. She tore off the paper when she was tucked up in bed. It was the snow dome!

24 Angelina shook the dome and hundreds of tiny snowflakes swirled around the ballerina. "It's the very best gift in the whole world!" she said happily.

christmas gifts

I just love Christmas, when it's cold and snowy outside, but we're warm and cosy inside. I can't wait to see my gift from Polly. I wonder what she has for Grandma and Grandpa?

Look carefully. Which of the little pictures can you see in the big one?

Write a tick ✓ or a cross ✗ in each box.

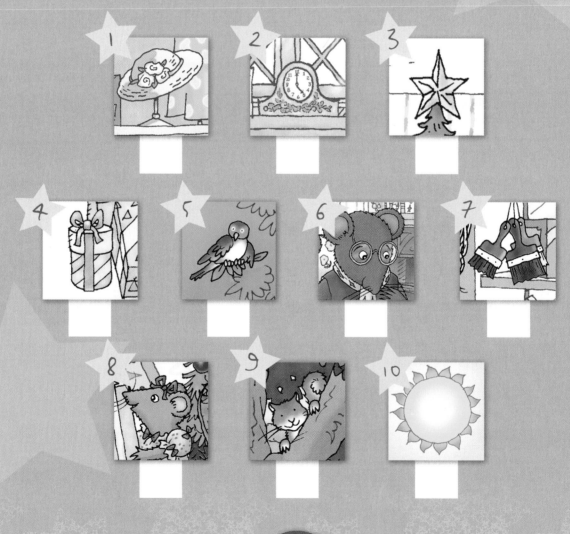

Angelina's dream

I have a special dream ... that one day I'll be a famous ballerina, just like my wonderful teacher, Miss Lilly!

Do you have a special dream? Draw and colour
in a picture of your dream, then write your name on the line.

My Special Dream

by ....

I hope you had fun
reading my annual. See you next year –
and I really hope your special dream comes true!